Thrills,
Spills, and
Cosmic Chills

For Judith and Zack. The truth is out there.
—*D.G.*

Thrills, Spills, and Cosmic Chills

by Dan Greenburg

illustrated by Macky Pamintuan

A STEPPING STONE BOOK™

Random House   New York

Text copyright © 2008 by Dan Greenburg
Illustrations copyright © 2008 by Macky Pamintuan

All rights reserved.
Published in the United States by Random House Children's Books,
a division of Random House, Inc., New York.

Random House and colophon are registered trademarks and A Stepping Stone
Book and colophon are trademarks of Random House, Inc.

Visit us on the Web!
www.steppingstonesbooks.com
www.randomhouse.com/kids

Educators and librarians, for a variety of teaching tools,
visit us at www.randomhouse.com/teachers

Library of Congress Cataloging-in-Publication Data
Greenburg, Dan.
Thrills, spills, and cosmic chills / by Dan Greenburg ;
illustrated by Macky Pamintuan. — 1st ed.
p.   cm. — (Weird planet ; 6)
"A Stepping Stone book."
Summary: While visiting Dizzyland near Los Angeles, Klatu, Lek, and Ploo, the
three alien siblings from the planet Loogl, find a fuzzy little alien named Mu
in the sideshow zoo of the amusement park and decide to set it free.
ISBN: 978-0-375-84337-2 (pbk.)
ISBN: 978-0-375-94337-9 (lib. bdg.)
[1. Extraterrestrial beings—Fiction. 2. Brothers and sisters—Fiction.
3. Amusement parks—Fiction. 4. Humorous stories. 5. Science fiction.]
I. Pamintuan, Macky, ill. II. Title.
PZ7.G8278Th 2008
[Fic]—dc22   2007023199

Printed in the United States of America
10 9 8 7 6 5 4 3 2 1
First Edition

Contents

Reach for the Sky, Yuh Mangy Varmint!

"Look at me, dudes," said Lek. He placed a big cowboy hat on his head and studied himself in the mirror. "Now I am a real cowpuncher," he said. "By the way, what *is* a *cowpuncher*?"

"Someone who makes a fist and hits cows," said Klatu.

"No, silly," said Lily. "*Cowpuncher* is just another word for *cowboy*."

"I knew that," said Klatu.

Klatu, Lek, and Ploo were alien kids from the planet Loogl. They'd crash-landed in the Nevada desert near Area 51, the secret army base. The rescue ship from planet Loogl was about to pick them up when guards from Area 51 came along. They should have returned home by now.

Klatu was the oldest. He had been flying the spaceship when it crashed. Lek was his younger brother, and Ploo was their younger sister. They all had large heads, big black eyes, gray skin, and antennas growing out of the middle of their heads.

If they had to, they could morph into human or animal shape for an *arp*. That's about an hour in Earth time. Just now Lek, Ploo, and Klatu had morphed into human shape.

"Do I look like a bad dude?" asked Lek, smiling in the mirror.

"The baddest of the bad dudes," said Lily. She was a human girl they had met when Ploo was a prisoner at Area 51.

Klatu, Lek, and Ploo were trying on cowboy outfits that smelled like an old lady's closet. They were about to get their pictures taken in the photo booth at West World. West World and Space World were part of a huge theme park in Los Angeles called Dizzyland. WHERE THE OLD WEST MEETS THE FUTURE said the signs.

"Thank you for taking us to Dizzyland, Jo-Jo," said Ploo.

"Oh, don't mention it," said Jo-Jo. She was a grown-up human who was helping them. She had once worked at Area 51. She was very good at fixing cars . . . and alien spaceships.

"Why should we not mention it?" Lek asked. "Will it get us into trouble?"

"No, no, that's just a saying," said Lily. "It means 'You're welcome.' "

As soon as the four kids got into their cowboy clothes, they went outside to have their pictures taken. Most days in Los Angeles were smoggy. Today the sun was so bright that shadows were sharp and colors snapped.

Just outside the dressing rooms was a street right out of the Old West. On both sides of a dirt road stood a bunch of one-story wooden buildings. They looked at least a hundred years old, but they were brand-new. There was a general store, a telegraph office, a newspaper office, a bank, and a blacksmith shop. Real horses were tied up outside the bank. They whinnied and snorted when the kids passed by.

Two huge motorized cowboy statues wheeled toward Lek, Ploo, and Klatu. "This town ain't big enough for both of us!" boomed a recording inside the first cowboy. "Reach for the sky, yuh mangy varmint!"

Lek and Klatu panicked and raised their hands high in the air.

"Hit the dirt, Bert!" boomed a recording in the second cowboy. Lek and Klatu dropped to the ground.

Lily and Jo-Jo giggled. Even Ploo thought it was funny.

"Reach for the sky, yuh mangy varmint!" said the first statue again.

Lek and Klatu jumped up again, hands in the air. Their clothes were brown from landing in the dirt.

"Guys, those cowboys aren't real," said Lily. "They're statues."

"I knew that," said Klatu, dusting himself off.

"I didn't," said Lek.

Klatu, Lek, Ploo, and Lily stood with the cowboys to have their pictures taken. When they were done, they returned the costumes and walked through a gate to Space World.

Space World had been built to seem like a town in the future. A monorail train zipped overhead along a gleaming silver track. Shiny silver buildings looked like they'd been designed years in the future. Fountains threw spurts of water in the air that seemed to float in space. Space World workers walked around in silver astronaut suits.

"Look!" shouted Klatu suddenly. "A spaceship!"

Everybody turned. A tall rocket stood on a launching pad, pointed at the stars.

"Maybe we could borrow it to fly back to planet Loogl!" said Lek excitedly.

"That there rocket isn't gonna fly you nowhere, hon," said Jo-Jo. "It's just a theme-park ride."

"Oh," said Lek.

Ploo held up her hand for quiet.

"What are you listening to?" Lily asked.

"A message asking for asking help," said Ploo. "I'm picking it up through E.S.P."

"I heard it, too," said Klatu. "You are not the only Loogling who has E.S.P., Ploo."

"The message is coming from over there," said Ploo, pointing.

Everyone turned in the direction Ploo was pointing. A sign said SPACE WORLD GALAXY ZOO. COME SEE CREATURES FROM ALL OVER THE UNIVERSE!

"That's a carnival sideshow, hon," said Jo-Jo. "They have lots of animals in cages. Some of them are pretty weird. I feel sorry for them, all cooped up like that."

"Let us walk that way," said Ploo. "Perhaps we can find out who is calling out for help."

Beware the
Growly-Voiced Man

Lek, Klatu, Ploo, Lily, and Jo-Jo walked down the long line of cages. Inside the cages were a bunch of odd creatures. There was a large white snake with two heads. There was an animal that looked like a bald monkey with a long tail and no fur at all. There was something with long hair hanging down from its head, covering its entire body. The cages smelled like rotten popcorn.

"That is the one who called for help," whispered Klatu. He pointed to the hairy creature.

"Are you sure?" asked Ploo. She looked at the hairy creature doubtfully.

"I am positive," said Klatu. He turned to the hairy creature. "How do you do?" he said. He spoke extra slowly and extra loudly. "My name is Klatu. Did you call for help?"

Lek punched Klatu in the arm. "You

varna!" whispered Lek. "If he esped a call for help, he does not want anybody to know!"

"Lek is right," said Lily.

"Do not listen to them," said Klatu to the hairy creature. "Tell me if you are the one who . . . *you* know what."

The hairy creature just stared at Klatu. The rotten popcorn smell grew stronger.

"I do not think this is the one who

esped for help," whispered Ploo. "I think it is that one over there." She nodded toward another cage.

Everyone looked at the cage. Inside was a small creature with soft brown fur, shiny black eyes, and the face of a baby gorilla.

"Aww," said Lily. "Look, Jo-Jo. It looks kind of like a baby gorilla. It's so *cute*! Do you think that's what it is? A baby gorilla?"

"I don't rightly know, darlin'," said Jo-Jo. "It sure is pretty, though."

"That is the prettiest thing I have ever seen," said Klatu.

"It may be pretty," said Lek. "But I wouldn't get close. It probably bites."

The prettiest thing Klatu has ever seen? thought Ploo. She looked closer at the creature. *Well, it might have soft brown fur, shiny black eyes, and a face like a baby gorilla. But it certainly does not have my velvety-soft gray skin or my lovely antenna curling out of my head.*

Hello, esped Ploo to the little animal. My name is Ploo. Did you call for help?

Yes, esped the creature. My name is Mu. Where do you come from? Ploo esped.

From far away, **said Mu.**

You mean from another country? Like Africa? said Ploo. She had learned about Africa in her Earthling Studies class.

From farther away than Africa, **said Mu.**

What's farther away than Africa? Ploo asked.

I come from another planet, **said Mu.**

You do? **said Ploo, getting excited.** Which one?

A planet called Vango 9, **said Mu.**

"Are you talking to that creature by E.S.P.?" asked Lily.

"Yes, she is," said Klatu. "I have heard the whole thing."

"What's the critter saying?" asked Jo-Jo.

"I shall tell you in a *mynt*," said Ploo.

"*I* could tell you right *now*," said Klatu.

Ploo returned to esping with Mu.

I have not heard of Vango 9, **she esped.**

Which wormhole did you come through, Mu?

The Delta Wormhole, said Mu. I landed near a place called Cincinnati. Do you know it?

Ploo turned to the others. "Where is Cincinnati?" she asked out loud.

"In Ohio, darlin'," said Jo-Jo. "Why?"

Soldiers captured me and took me to an air-force base, Mu esped.

The same thing happened to me at Area 51! esped Ploo. My brothers and I came from planet Loogl. How did you escape?

I did not escape, said Mu. I was stolen from the base by a man who worked there. He sold me to people who buy strange animals for carnivals. The man who runs this sideshow bought me. He is as mean as the man who sold me. No, worse. Can you help me get out of this cage?

Ploo had been jealous of Mu's beauty at first. But when she heard the little space traveler's sad story, she forgot about her jealousy.

Mu, we will try to come up with a plan to help you, said Ploo.

Oh, thank you! said Mu. But it will have to be— Uh-oh.

What is it? said Ploo.

Here comes the man who brought me here! said Mu. Do not let him see you talking to me!

A tall man in jeans, cowboy boots, and a big black cowboy hat strolled over to Ploo. He had a dark beard and a nasty scar on his face. "Howdy, little lady," said the man in a growly voice.

"Howdy," said Ploo.

"I wouldn't get too close to that there critter," said the man with the growly voice. "She's mean as a snake. Plus which, she bites."

"I *told* you she bites, did I not?" said Lek.

"She does not look mean to *me*," said
Ploo.

"Yeah? Well, looks can fool yuh," said
the man. "Yuh get too close to that little
creep, she'll take your arm right off. Then
your mom here will sue me." He turned to
Jo-Jo with a sly smile. "That right, Mom?"

"That's right," said Jo-Jo.

"Where yuh from?" asked the man. He looked at each of them closely.

"Hollyhocks," said Klatu.

"Vegas," said Jo-Jo.

"That so?" said the man. "Well, I'm too polite to call yuh liars, but I'm real good with accents. And I doubt that any of yuh are from either Vegas or Hollyhocks. Mom, yuh sound like you're from Texas. And your youngsters sound like they're from way farther away than Vegas. *Way* farther."

He suspects something, Ploo esped. *It is not safe for us to talk to him.*

Ploo is right, esped Mu. *You must leave before he finds out you are aliens. Unless you want to end up in a cage like me.*

Klatu felt a sudden tightness in his head. How long had it been since they'd morphed into human shape? Almost an *arp*. They would morph back into Looglish shape any *mynt* now! It would not be good for this man to see them with their big heads, huge black eyes, gray skin, and antennas!

Also, Klatu's English-language gum was losing its flavor. It was getting harder and harder for him to speak.

"I have . . . much hunger," said Klatu. "Is it not the time that we . . . should do the eating of lunch?" Now Klatu felt a sharp pain in his forehead. His antenna was about to burst right through his skin.

"It's only ten o'clock in the morning," said the man. "Yuh eat lunch that early where yuh come from, pardner?"

"Klatu's a growin' boy," said Jo-Jo. "C'mon, kids, let's go get us some grub."

"Say, what kind of a name is Klatu?" asked the man.

3

Klatu Is Not a Scaredy-<u>Ketzelongo</u>

They slipped away from the growly-voiced man in the nick of time. Just as they were crossing back into West World, first Klatu, then Lek, then Ploo burst out of their human shapes and into their Looglish ones. They ducked behind the telegraph office to finish their morphing.

Ploo got out the language gum. The green gum balls were for English. She and her brothers chewed them up.

"Whew! That was close!" said Lek. "We almost morphed right in front of that man. We would have been doomed!"

"Y'all better morph back into human shape fast," said Jo-Jo.

"We cannot do it so fast," said Ploo. "We should wait awhile between morphings. Otherwise it will be painful. And tiring."

"What if somebody sees us like this?" said Klatu. "What should we say?"

Just then a man, a woman, and a little boy came around the corner of the telegraph office. When they saw Klatu, Lek, and Ploo, they gasped.

"I just *love* these alien costumes we bought at Space World," said Ploo.

"Me too," said Klatu. "These costumes almost make us look like *real aliens*."

"Boy, you can say *that* again!" said the man.

"Okay, I will," said Klatu. "These costumes almost make us look like *real aliens*."

The man, the woman, and the little boy walked away. They went to find the store that sold such great costumes.

"I am worried about poor Mu," said Ploo. "We need to come up with a plan to rescue her."

"What if we come back here tonight after the park closes?" said Ploo. "We could climb over the fence, open her cage, and set her free."

"That's much too dangerous," said Jo-Jo. "I will not have y'all doing anything like that."

"But, Jo-Jo, we can't just leave her here," said Lily.

"Maybe we could try to buy her from that man or somethin'," said Jo-Jo.

"Yeah," said Lily. "Like *that* would work."

All of them tried to think of ways to save poor Mu.

When they walked around the other side of the telegraph office, they saw a strange sight. Inside a fenced-in space, a chubby man was sitting on something that bucked and lurched and threatened to throw him off. Finally, it did. The chubby man landed hard on the ground.

"What is that terrible thing he was sitting on?" asked Lek.

Jo-Jo laughed. "It's called a mechanical bull, darlin'. People try to ride them, just like they were in the rodeo."

"I would not sit on that bull if you paid me fifty *gorins*!" said Lek.

"You are a scaredy-*ketzelongo*," said Klatu. "I would do it for nothing."

"You would not last three *sikkens* on that bull," said Lek.

"Watch me!" said Klatu.

Lek, Lily, Jo-Jo, and Ploo took a seat on the fence. Klatu ran over to the mechanical bull and climbed up on it. A man in cowboy clothes was in charge of the bull. He looked at Klatu and frowned.

"You shouldn't be ridin' this thing, pardner," said the man.

"Why not?" asked Klatu.

"Well, you're not really big enough," said the man. "And that space-alien costume you're wearing is gonna get in your way."

"Oh, I can ride this thing," said Klatu. "I have done it many times where I come from."

"Where do you come from?" asked the man.

Klatu had to think about that. "Dulles," said Klatu.

"Dulles?" said the man. "Where's that at?"

"Dulles, in the great state of Taxes," said Klatu.

"You mean *Dallas,* in the great state of *Texas*?" said the man.

"That is what I said. Now are you going to let me ride it or not?" Klatu asked.

The man laughed. "Whatever you say, pardner."

The man flipped a switch and the mechanical bull began bucking. On the first buck, Klatu went sailing into the air. He landed hard in the dirt.

Jo-Jo, Lily, Lek, and Ploo rushed over to him.

"Are you okay, darlin'?" Jo-Jo asked.

"Of course I am," said Klatu. He painfully picked himself off the ground. He brushed the dirt off his clothes.

"I thought you said you could ride

that thing," said Lek. "You did not last even one *sikken*."

"My darn space-alien costume got in the way," said Klatu.

Lek, Klatu, Ploo, Lily, and Jo-Jo walked down the main street of West World. Two horses were still tied up outside the newspaper office. There was a faint smell of horse manure as they passed. The kids wrinkled up their noses.

"How are we going to rescue poor Mu?" Ploo asked.

"We could dress her up like a cowgirl and sneak her out of here," said Klatu.

"Klatu, that makes no sense," said Lily.

"Why?" asked Klatu.

"Where would you find a cowgirl outfit that small?" said Lily. "How could you sneak a cowgirl outfit into her cage?"

"How could you ever make a baby gorilla look like a little girl?" asked Jo-Jo.

"She is not a baby gorilla," said Ploo. "She is a creature from Vango 9."

"Uh-oh," said Lek. He was looking over his shoulder.

"What is it?" said Klatu.

"The man with the growly voice," Lek whispered. "I think he is following us."

"Oh, Lek, you are seeing things that are not there," said Klatu.

Lek was still looking over his shoulder. "I am almost positive it is the man with the growly voice," he said. "How can we get rid of him?"

"Maybe we could lose him on Pikes Peak," said Jo-Jo. "That ride always has swarms of people around it."

"Isn't Pikes Peak a mountain in Colorado?" asked Lily.

"Yep, but it's also a roller coaster here in West World," said Jo-Jo. "It's kind of scary. The kids call it Pikes Puke. It might be a good way to lose the growly-voiced man, though. If he's really followin' us, that is. How do y'all feel about goin' on a scary roller coaster?"

"I am not afraid of *anything,*" said Klatu proudly.

"I am afraid of *everything,*" said Lek. "But I am willing to ride it to lose the growly-voiced man."

"Well, I don't know if he's followin' us or not," said Jo-Jo. "But if he is, I reckon we better hustle our buns over to that roller coaster."

4

Going Down . . . and Up . . . and Down

"I am really going to hate this, right?" said Lek.

He sat down in the first car of the roller coaster next to Klatu and Ploo. Jo-Jo and Lily took seats behind them.

"Nah," said Jo-Jo, "this is a piece of cake."

"You mean it will have a creamy center and get crumbs and icing all over my face?" asked Klatu.

"No, hon," said Jo-Jo. "That's just a saying. It means it will be easy."

"I knew that," said Klatu.

A woman in a fringed leather cowgirl outfit walked up to them. She pulled a heavy padded bar down across their chests.

"I sure do like those space-alien costumes of yours," said the woman. "Where'd you get them?"

"At Space World," said Ploo.

"That's funny," said the woman. "I worked at Space World till last Thursday. I never saw any like yours."

"Uh, they just got these in today," said Klatu.

"Then that explains it," the woman said. "Okay, guys, hold on tight. And whatever you do, don't stand up or stick your arms or legs outside of the car."

"Do not worry," said Lek. "I will not even do that when the ride is over."

The woman smiled. She thought Lek was joking. He wasn't.

The roller coaster jolted into motion.

"I am scared," said Lek.

The roller coaster moved forward. It turned a corner and began to climb a hill. Slowly, slowly, the roller coaster cranked up the hill. The view from the hill looked like the real Pikes Peak in Colorado. There were rock walls made out of plaster, and fake snow.

"You know," said Lek, "this does not seem so bad after all. I think I was worried for nothing."

The roller coaster reached the top of the first hill. The drop-off was so steep that Klatu, Lek, and Ploo could barely see the tracks on the way down.

"Forget what I just said," Lek whispered. "I want to get off now, okay? I am getting off right now. I am . . . I am . . . I . . . I . . . IIIIIIIIIIIIIIIIIIIIIIIIIIIIIIIIIIIIIIIIIIIIIIIIIIIIIIIIII!"

Lek's scream was joined by the others' as the car plunged downward. It felt as though they'd left their stomachs at the top of the hill. The instant the roller coaster hit the bottom of the hill, it turned sharply to the right.

"Is that it?" asked Lek. "Can we get off now?"

The roller coaster started cranking slowly up the next hill.

"We do not seem to be getting off," said Lek.

When the roller coaster reached the top of the hill, the drop-off was even steeper than the one before. And when it raced to the bottom of the hill, it twisted and lurched and then turned upside down!

"Oh no!" Lek screamed. "This is worse than the growly-voiced man! I want to go back and find the growly-voiced man!"

When the roller coaster finally shuddered to a stop, Lek was stuck to his seat like a bug on a windshield. Ploo and Klatu gently peeled him off and helped him out of the car.

"Want to ride again, Lek?" asked Klatu.

Lek just glared at him.

When they came out of the Pikes Peak exit, they looked nervously in all directions. The growly-voiced man was nowhere in sight.

"Okay," said Lek. "It looks like we lost him. Now we can go back to having fun. No more roller coasters!"

They walked along the main street of the fake Western town. They began trying to think of ways to rescue Mu from her cage again.

Ploo tried to picture Mu's little face. She certainly was pretty.

"That Mu is really pretty, is she not?" said Ploo.

"She certainly is," said Klatu.

"Do you think she is . . . ?" Ploo began.

"Do we think she is what?" Lily asked.

"Prettier than I am?" Ploo finished. The second she asked that, she wished she hadn't. She felt embarrassed.

"I think you are *much* prettier than she is," said Lek.

"I think you are almost exactly as pretty as she is," said Klatu.

"Thanks a lot, Klatu," said Ploo. "Now, how can we get Mu out of that cage?"

"Maybe we could bake her a cake with a little saw inside it," said Lily. "Then she could saw her way out."

"Why would she need to saw her way out of the cake?" Klatu asked. "How would she even get inside of it?"

"I meant she could saw her way out of the *cage,* not the cake," said Lily.

"Oh," said Klatu.

"Maybe we could all get jobs at Space World," said Lek. "Then we could let her out with our keys."

It was almost dark out. Lights all over Dizzyland had winked on. A few crickets had started to chirp in the bushes.

Klatu, Lek, Ploo, Jo-Jo, and Lily had spent the rest of the day in the park. They ate ice cream and cotton candy. They ate Popsicles, and Klatu ate the Popsicle sticks inside them. They rode the Space Needle and the Whirling Space Wheel. The Whirling Space Wheel was just like the machine that trains astronauts to live in space. It whirls around so fast, it makes them throw up.

They were still trying to think of ways to rescue Mu. From time to time, one of them thought they saw the growly-voiced man. They were pretty sure about it now. He was following them.

"Now that it is dark," said Lek, "it will be easier for the growly-voiced man to jump out and attack us."

"I think we'd better get you guys back to the hotel for dinner," said Jo-Jo.

"We have not yet come up with a plan to rescue Mu," said Ploo.

"We will have to think about that back at the hotel," said Jo-Jo. "C'mon, kids."

"I still think we should come back late tonight and try to rescue her," said Ploo.

Jo-Jo shook her head. "I told y'all that's much too dangerous. We will just have to think of another way."

There is no other way, Ploo esped to Lek and Klatu. After Jo-Jo has gone to sleep, we must come back here and free Mu.

No, Jo-Jo is right, Lek esped. It is much too dangerous. If we do that, they will catch us. The growly-voiced man will kill us! Or he will at least lock us in a cage. We will never see planet Loogl or our family again!

I think coming back here tonight is a fine idea, esped Klatu. Lek, you are a fraidy-ketzelongo!

And you are a varna! esped Lek.

Klatu, Lek, Ploo, Lily, and Jo-Jo started toward the front gate.

When we get back to the hotel, Ploo esped, pretend you are very tired. Pretend you want to go to bed right away. When Jo-Jo goes to sleep, we will sneak out and come back to rescue Mu.

We are actors, said Klatu. Actors are great pretenders.

"So what did you think of Dizzyland?" Jo-Jo asked.

"Dizzyland is a fun place," said Klatu. "Except for the growly-voiced man."

"And except for the roller coaster," said Lek.

No Fun, No Fish, Just Sleep

As soon as they got back to their room at the Beverly Hills Hotel, Klatu stretched his arms up and yawned loudly.

"Well, that was a fun day," he said. "But, boy, am I sleepy!"

"Me too," said Ploo. "I can hardly keep my eyes open."

"Me either," said Lek.

"Me either," said Lily. "I think I'll go straight to bed."

"But we haven't even had dinner yet," said Jo-Jo. "You *never* want to go to bed early. Why are y'all so sleepy?"

"Well, Dizzyland tired us out," said Klatu. "I am exalted."

"Do you mean *exhausted*?" Jo-Jo asked.

"That too," said Klatu. "We must all go to bed now." He made loud yawning noises.

"What's going on here, kids?" asked Jo-Jo. "This is beginning to sound pretty fishy to me."

"*Nothing* is going on," said Klatu. "No fish. Why would we have fish? We hate fish."

"That's just a saying," said Lily. "*Fishy* means Jo-Jo thinks we're up to something funny." She opened her eyes wide and gave Jo-Jo an innocent look.

"Nothing funny," said Klatu. "No fun. No fish. Just sleep."

"Okay, then," said Jo-Jo. "As soon as we have dinner, y'all can go to bed."

For dinner, they ate pepperoni pizza and ice cream. Klatu also ate the box the pizza came in. He loved pizza boxes even more than pizza.

Right after dinner, the kids washed up and got ready for bed. Lily closed the heavy glass door to the terrace and drew the blinds.

"Good night, Jo-Jo," said Lily, yawning loudly. "Are you going to bed now, too?"

"No, darlin', I'm not sleepy," said Jo-Jo.

"You *look* sleepy," said Klatu.

"Yes. Very sleepy," said Lek. "You look like you can hardly keep your eyes open."

"Well, I feel very wide awake," said Jo-Jo. "I may get into bed, but I think I'm gonna read for a while."

"Oh, reading is very bad for you," said

Klatu. "Reading will ruin your eyes."

"Really?" said Jo-Jo. "I don't think that's at all true."

"Oh yes," said Lek. "When people on planet Loogl read too much, their eyes begin to hurt. Then they drop out and fall on the ground."

"I promise to stop reading before my eyes drop out and fall on the ground, darlin'," said Jo-Jo. She hugged and kissed every one of them. "Good night, y'all."

It took a long time till Jo-Jo got tired. It took even longer till she turned off her reading light. As soon as they heard her begin to snore, the kids crept out of bed. Jo-Jo's mouth was open and she was making sounds like snuffling pigs.

"Let's go," Lily whispered.

"What if Jo-Jo wakes up and finds that we are gone?" Lek asked.

"Look at her," said Lily. "Do you think she'll wake up before morning?"

The kids all shook their heads.

"First we should morph into human shape," said Ploo.

"Good idea," said Klatu. "All right, guys. Ready to morph?"

"Ready," said Ploo.

"Ready," said Lek.

"One, two, three . . . morph!" said Klatu.

With a soft sound like a sigh, the three Loogling kids grew outward and upward. Their heads grew smaller. Their arms and legs grew thicker. Their eyes shrank down to beady little human size.

They left their hotel room and took the elevator to the first floor. The lobby was quiet and empty of guests. The man behind the desk looked half asleep. His eyelids kept

fluttering closed, then snapping open.

Just outside the hotel, a cab was wait-ing. Ploo, Klatu, Lek, and Lily got in and slammed the door behind them. To pay for the cab, Lily had brought along a bag of coins they'd won in Las Vegas.

"Where you kids going?" asked the driver. He had a shaggy red beard and a Los Angeles Dodgers cap.

"The Dizzyland theme park, please," said Lily.

"I hate to spoil your fun, guys," said the driver. "But Dizzyland is closed now."

"Oh, we know that," said Klatu. "We work there."

"Really?" said the driver.

"Sure," said Lily. "We have keys to get in and everything." She held up her room key.

"Well, that's different," said the driver. "If you work there, I guess it's okay, then. I must say, though, you look a little young to be working there."

"Oh, we're a lot older than we look," said Lily. "How old do you think we look?"

The driver turned around in his seat and studied them, frowning. "I'd say you girls are . . . about ten. And the boys? Maybe . . . twelve and sixteen."

Klatu, Lek, Ploo, and Lily all roared with laughter.

"Twelve and sixteen! Ha-ha! That is a good one!" said Klatu. "My brother Lek here is twenty-eight. And I am thirty-four."

"I find that pretty hard to believe," said the driver.

"Klatu is kidding," said Ploo. "We girls are sixteen, and the boys are eighteen and nineteen. Why would we want to go to Dizzyland when they are closed unless we worked there?"

"I guess you have a point," said the driver. "All right, then."

A Dangerous Plan
to Save Mu

The cab took off. It went down Sunset Boulevard, past rows of palm trees. It passed the tall hedges that hid the homes of the rich people of Beverly Hills. It went down the freeway, past the homes of the not-so-rich and the poor of central and downtown Los Angeles. It went through an area with no homes at all. It looked dark and lonely out there. The cab pulled up outside the front gate of Dizzyland.

"Here we are," said the driver. "Dizzy-land. Where the Old West meets the future." He looked at the meter. "That'll be twenty dollars."

Klatu, Lek, and Ploo looked startled. They turned to Lily.

"Is twenty dollars a lot of money?" whispered Ploo.

"Yes," said Lily. "But I think I have enough."

She took out her bag filled with coins. She gave it to the driver.

"Holy cow," said the driver. "Is this all the money you kids have?"

"Oh no," said Lily. "We have another bag to get home on."

"It's going to take me a while to count this," said the driver.

"That's okay," said Lily. "We don't have to be at work for another ten minutes."

The driver counted the coins. It took him almost five minutes. He handed a few coins back.

"You gave me too much," he said. "This is what was left over. Fourteen pennies."

"Well, then, please take that as your tip," said Lily.

"Oh, thank you," said the driver. "You kids don't take cabs much, do you?"

"Not that much," said Lily.

"I could tell," said the driver.

Klatu, Lek, Ploo, and Lily got out of the cab. They walked up to the front gate. It was very dark and very quiet on the other side of the gate. In the moonlight, they could barely make out the shapes of the roller coaster and the rocket ride. Both looked kind of spooky in the dark.

They tried the handle on the gate. Sure enough, it was locked. They walked back

along the high iron fence, looking for a place to get through. They heard the sound of crickets in the bushes and bugs that sounded like tiny electric saws.

"Should we climb over the fence or tunnel under it?" Lek asked.

"Climb over it," said Ploo.

Ten yards from the front gate, the fence was a little lower. They carefully climbed up to the top and swung their legs over. As they got ready to climb down the other side, they saw that the cab had not left. The driver was looking up at them on top of the fence.

"I thought you guys told me you had keys!" the driver called.

"We do!" said Klatu. "But they are the wrong ones!"

"Oh," said the driver. "All right." He shrugged and drove away.

"I do not think he believed you," said Lek. "I feel like a *varna*."

"That does not matter now," said Ploo. "What matters is that we find Mu and set her free."

"Before it is too late," said Lek.

Klatu, Lek, Ploo, and Lily scrambled down the fence.

To their left, they saw the outline of the Pikes Peak roller-coaster track. That was West World. To their right, they saw the outline of the Whirling Space Wheel. That was Space World.

They took off to their right. There were no lights and only a sliver of moon. It was hard not to bump into things, but Looglings could see better than humans in the dark. Ploo took Lily's hand to guide her. It had been almost fifty *mynts* since they'd left the hotel. They began morphing back into their alien shapes.

When they reached the row of cages in the Space World sideshow, all of the creatures were asleep.

"Which cage is Mu in?" Lily whispered.

"The one at the other end of the Galaxy Zoo, I think," said Ploo. "I will try to reach her by E.S.P."

Mu! Ploo esped. Wake up! It is me, Ploo.

And my brothers, Lek and Klatu. And my friend Lily. We have come to rescue you!

There was only silence.

"Nothing," said Ploo sadly.

"Perhaps she is sleeping," said Klatu.

"Perhaps she is dead," said Lek.

"If we cannot get an answer, we have come all this way for nothing," said Klatu.

"And now we will not even be able to return to our hotel," said Lek. "The growly-voiced man will catch us and put us all into cages. We will never see our poor parents again!"

Wake up, Mu! Ploo esped. *We have come to rescue you!*

Silence.

"We are doomed," said Lek. "I am too young to die."

"No, you are just the right age to die," said Klatu.

Ploo! esped a voice. *I cannot believe you have come back to help me!*

Ploo, Lek, and Klatu practically shouted for joy.

I told you we would come back, Ploo esped.

Just then they heard a frightening sound. Growling. They couldn't tell where it was coming from.

"What is that terrible sound?" Lek asked.

"It sounds like a guard dog," said Lily.

"There she is!" said Klatu. "Hi, Mu!"

Ahead was Mu's cage. Her friendly little face peered out at them from behind the bars. In the dim light, Ploo could see it clearly. Ploo told herself once more she wasn't jealous of Mu's beauty. But deep down inside, she might be—a little.

You were very brave to come, Mu esped. *But it is dangerous to be here at night. Beware of the guard dogs!*

Ploo, Klatu, and Lek knelt down and tried to find a lock or a handle on the outside of Mu's cage. There didn't seem to be either.

Mu, tell us how to open your cage, Ploo esped.

All right, Mu esped. There are two hinges at the end of the door. Do you see them?

Yes, Ploo esped.

I cannot reach them from in here, said Mu. But you could. Can you lift them out?

I will try, said Klatu. He bent down and tried to pry the hinges out of their holders. They were rusted and didn't move.

Suddenly they heard a loud voice calling from the front entrance.

"Hey! Is somebody in the park?"

It is the man who bought me! Mu esped. Hurry, Klatu! Remove those hinges!

"It's the growly-voiced man!" said Lily.

"We are doomed!" cried Lek.

7

Midnight Snacks

"Hurry, Klatu!" said Lily.

"I am trying," said Klatu. "Help me!"

Ploo and Lek ran to Klatu and grabbed the hinges, too.

"Is there somebody over by the creature cages?" shouted the growly-voiced man.

Ploo's long fingers shook with fright. She could barely grip the hinges.

"Can you do this any faster?" asked Lily.

"We are doing the best we can," said Ploo.

"We will never make it!" said Lek.

Somehow the three Looglings pried the first hinge loose. And then the second. Klatu tore at the cage door.

It fell to the cement with a loud *CLANG*. Mu scrambled out of the cage.

"Who goes there?" shouted the growly-voiced man. "Halt! Yuh are trespassing on private property!"

"Run!" said Ploo.

Ploo, Lily, Lek, and Klatu tore off in the direction of West World. Little Mu followed close behind. The growly-voiced man ran after them.

"Yuh can run all yuh like, but there's no way out of here!" shouted the growly-voiced man. "Yuh are trapped!"

"Oh no! We're trapped!" cried Lek.

"If yuh stop now, I'll go easy on yuh!" shouted the growly-voiced man. "If yuh keep on running, I'll show yuh no mercy when I catch yuh!"

"Oh no! He will show us no mercy when he catches us!" cried Lek. "Maybe we should stop!"

"He is just trying to scare us," said Ploo. "Keep running!"

They ran and they ran. They ran past the rocket ride. They ran past the entrance to the monorail. They were getting short of breath.

They crossed over into West World. They ran down the main street of the old Western

town. They ran past the telegraph office, where the man and woman and their little boy had almost caught them morphing. They ran past the place where Klatu had ridden the bull. They ran past the entrance to the Pikes Peak roller coaster.

Lily felt as though her lungs were bursting. Klatu, Lek, and Ploo felt as though their *klopotskis* were bursting. They ran past the newspaper office. Ploo's twin hearts were beating as fast as a hummingbird's. She stopped and tried the door. It wasn't locked.

"In here!" Ploo whispered.

Klatu, Lek, Lily, Ploo, and Mu slipped inside. They closed the door behind them. They ducked below the windows so the growly-voiced man couldn't see them. A moment later, they heard him run noisily past the newspaper office.

They waited in silence for several minutes. The only sound was that of their breathing.

"I think he's gone," said Lily.

"We are safe!" said Lek.

"Mu, you are free!" said Ploo.

Mu looked at the kids who had just saved her life. She growled.

Klatu, Lek, Ploo, and Lily stared at Mu. Somehow, this was not how they'd expected to be thanked. Mu growled again, even louder. It was the sound they'd heard when they first reached the cages. The sound they'd thought was a guard dog.

In the dim light of the fake newspaper office, they watched Mu's cute little baby gorilla face begin to change. Mu's adorable eyes glowed red. Long claws sprouted out of her hands. She opened her mouth and showed her teeth. They grew long and sharp.

What is happening to Mu? **Klatu esped.**

I do not know, **esped Ploo.** Mu, what is happening to you?

<u>Nothing</u> is happening to me, **Mu esped.** I am from Vango 9. This is how we look when we are hungry. I have not eaten meat in weeks.

"Are you talking to Mu by E.S.P.?" Lily asked.

"Yes," said Lek.

"What is she saying?"

"You would not be happy to know that," said Lek.

Mu, we can find a place to buy you meat as soon as we get out of Dizzyland, **Ploo esped.**

We do not need to find a place to buy me meat, **Mu esped.** I have all the meat I need right here.

8

Lions and Tigers and Bears, Oh My!

"I do not feel so well," said Lek.

"What is happening?" Lily asked. She grabbed Klatu's arm.

"Nothing good," said Lek. He figured Lily could guess what was happening.

Like a giant python, Mu unhinged her lower jaw. Her mouth opened wide enough to swallow any of their heads.

I have an idea, Klatu esped.

What is your idea? said Ploo.

Run! said Klatu.

Klatu tore out of the newspaper office at full speed. Lek, Ploo, and Lily ran right behind him.

They raced down the main street of West World in the opposite direction. They ran past the entrance to the Pikes Peak roller coaster. They ran past the place where Klatu had ridden the bull. They ran past the telegraph office, where the man and woman and their little boy had almost caught them morphing.

They couldn't tell if they were getting ahead of Mu or if she was gaining on them. They were feeling short of breath again. It wasn't a warm night, but Lily's skin was bathed in sweat. Klatu tripped over a rock and fell.

Lek and Lily yanked him back on his feet and they continued running. They ran past the West World fun house.

"In here!" Ploo whispered.

Klatu, Lek, Lily, and Ploo slipped inside.

It was very dark inside the fun house. A line of tiny red bulbs along the floor was the only lighting.

"I think we lost her!" said Klatu.

"But she might have seen us come inside," said Lek.

"It's creepy in here," said Lily. "I can't see a thing."

From somewhere nearby, they heard a creaking sound. Then they heard an eerie groan.

"My E.S.P. is picking up some strange thoughts," said Ploo. "I fear that some evil creature may be hiding in here."

"What kind of thoughts are you picking up?" asked Lily.

"Nasty ones," said Ploo. "Something with huge jaws like Earth dinosaurs. Long, powerful hind legs. Short front legs with scary claws. Glowing green eyes."

"Huge jaws like Earth dinosaurs? Short front legs with scary claws? Glowing green eyes?" said Lek.

"Yes!" said Ploo.

"Oh, sorry," said Lek. "Those thoughts you picked up were *mine*. I was just worrying about what kind of monsters we might find in here."

Suddenly a light snapped on. In front of them loomed four giant creatures. Some of them had tremendous heads. Everybody screamed.

"Jumping *jeblonskies*! It is the monsters from my thoughts!" Lek shouted.

They turned and started running back toward the entrance.

"Wait!" said Ploo.

Everybody turned around to look at her.

"What?" said Lily.

"Those monsters are *us*!" said Ploo.

"What are you saying?" asked Klatu.

"Those monsters are just reflections of *us*! In a big mirror!" said Ploo, pointing.

"Ploo's right," said Lily.

A big fun-house mirror covered the wall. The curved mirror distorted their reflections. It made them look lots bigger and very scary.

"I knew that," said Klatu.

"If you knew that, then why did you run away?" Ploo asked.

"To make you not feel like the only stupid ones," said Klatu.

"Shhh!" Lek said.

Everyone stopped talking. They heard a noise at the front entrance. The front door creaked slowly open. Someone—or something—crept inside.

Lek, Klatu, Ploo, and Lily froze. They didn't dare make a sound.

First there was silence. Then the sound of footsteps.

Mu crept around a corner.

Her eyes glowed red in the dark. A deep growl came out of her chest. Her mouth opened, revealing long white fangs that dripped with slime. Once more, her lower jaw unhinged like a python's. They were trapped between the large mirror in one direction and Mu in the other!

Mu's mouth opened wide again.

Lek whimpered.

I just had another idea, guys, **Klatu esped.**

Careful, **Ploo warned.** Mu can read your thoughts.

I know that, **Klatu esped.** All right, here is my idea: An Earthling lion. An Earthling tiger. An Earthling grizzly bear. Do you understand?

Yes! **Lek esped.**

Yes! **Ploo esped.**

Morphing to wild animals so soon after they had been humans would be painful and exhausting. But they had to try it or Mu would eat them!

Good, **Klatu esped.** Ready, guys? One . . . two . . . three!

The moment Klatu counted to three, he and Lek and Ploo began to morph.

Klatu's head creaked and groaned and then cracked like an eggshell. A bigger furry head sprang out of it. His new furry head was tan. It had fangs and a heavy brown mane. His body grew much longer. He had paws the size of dust mops. A long tail with a large tuft of brown fur swished at the end.

"Ow!" cried Klatu, but it came out more like a lion's growl.

Lek's human form disappeared as well. In its place grew an orange-and-black-striped face and a large orange-and-black-striped body.

"Ouch!" cried Lek, but it sounded more like a tiger's snarl.

Ploo's face was replaced by a dog-like snout and a mouth full of sharp white teeth. Her skin was covered in brown fur. Her body kept growing and growing till it was larger than either of the others.

"Oof!" cried Ploo, but it sounded more like the grunt of a grizzly bear.

Mu backed away from them. The red glow was gone from her eyes. She no longer bared her fangs or claws.

Ploo got up on her hind legs. And then so did Lek and Klatu. The three of them roared so loudly, the ground shook.

We eat meat, too, Mu! Ploo esped.

You would not even be a horse doover for us! esped Klatu.

Are you trying to say hors d'oeuvre? esped Ploo. I think it means appetizer in French.

I knew that, said Klatu.

Mu trembled with fear.

I am so s-sorry! Mu esped. I m-m-made a t-terrible mistake. It would be wrong to try and eat a Loogling. I see that now.

Really? said Lek. He loved the feeling of being a powerful Bengal tiger. Would you not even like to try a nibble?

N-no, I have only respect for Looglings, said Mu. M-may I leave now?

We will be glad to escort you back to your cage, said Ploo.

Actually, I was hoping to go to the front gate, said Mu.

The front gate is not a choice, said Lek. Back to your cage, or stay for dinner. Our *dinner. That is the choice.* He roared loudly.

Then going back to my cage might be nice, esped Mu.

Good choice, said Lek.

On the way back to Space World, they ran into the growly-voiced man. Mu looked like a baby gorilla again. When the growly-voiced man saw Mu, Lily, the lion, the tiger, and the giant grizzly bear, his jaw almost hit the ground.

"Wh-what are yuh d-doing with Mu?" he asked. He tried to sound angry, but his voice kept breaking like a teenage boy's. And he couldn't hide his trembling.

"We're taking her back to her cage," said Lily. "You got a *problem* with that, chief?"

"N-no," said the growly-voiced man. "No problem at all."

We Didn't Go
Anywhere, We
Didn't Do Anything

"'You got a *problem* with that, chief?'" Ploo repeated. She giggled tiredly. "Lily, you are certainly one tough little Earthling."

"Especially when I've got a lion, a tiger, and a grizzly bear for friends," said Lily.

It was an hour later, and the same cab-driver was taking them back to the Beverly Hills Hotel. He'd been worried about them and returned to Dizzyland to make sure they were all right. Luckily, Lek, Klatu, and Ploo had just finished morphing back to human shape.

Now they were exhausted. Their bodies ached from so much shape-changing, so Lek, Ploo, and Klatu were lying down on the cab seats.

"You kids sure look tired," said the cab-driver.

"Sometimes we work too hard at our jobs," said Lek.

When the cab dropped the four kids back in front of the hotel, Lily gave the driver her second bag of coins.

"This may not be enough," said Lily. "But if you wait, I'll go up to our room and get some more from Jo-Jo. She's our grown-up friend."

"That's okay," said the driver. "I get the feeling you might have forgotten to tell Jo-Jo you were going to Dizzyland. I don't want to get you guys in trouble."

The kids dragged themselves tiredly into the hotel lobby and took an elevator up to their floor. When they reached their room, Lily stopped them before they unlocked the door.

"Shhhh," she said. "We'd better be super quiet, guys. If Jo-Jo wakes up and finds out we went to Dizzyland, she'll have kittens."

"Ohhh, I would so much like to see that," said Klatu. "I *love* kittens."

"*Having kittens* is just a saying," said Lily. "It means she'll really be mad at us."

"Okay, then, let us not wake her," said Lek.

Klatu unlocked the door and they crept inside. They listened carefully. From somewhere came the sound of snuffling pigs. Jo-Jo was still snoring. Ploo motioned them forward.

As they tiptoed past Jo-Jo's room, Klatu tripped on a rug, slid across the floor, and crashed into a coffee table. A glass vase full of flowers crashed to the floor.

"Klatu, you *varna!*" said Lek. "Now look what you have done!"

"Klatu?" called Jo-Jo. "What was that noise?" She walked sleepily to the door of her room.

"A vase fell onto the floor by itself," said Klatu. "I think the flowers in it were too heavy."

"What are you kids doing up at this hour?" Jo-Jo asked. "Y'all didn't go out, did you?"

"Yes," said Lek, who could not lie. "We did go out."

"I sure hope y'all didn't go outside of the hotel," said Jo-Jo.

"Would that have made you angry?" Klatu asked.

"That would have made me boiling mad," said Jo-Jo.

"Boiling mad?" said Klatu.

"Boiling mad," said Jo-Jo.

"In that case," said Klatu, "we only went downstairs to the lobby to buy some ice cream. I would not like to see you hot and bubbling and turning to steam."

"Since we're all awake," said Jo-Jo, "maybe we should talk about ways we can rescue Mu."

Lek, Klatu, Ploo, and Lily looked at each other.

"We talked to Mu by E.S.P. while you were sleeping," said Ploo. "She changed her mind about being rescued. She decided she would miss the other animals at the sideshow too much if she left."

"Really?" said Jo-Jo. "I thought she was miserable there."

"Oh no," said Klatu. "Not miserable at all. She just didn't think they served enough meat there. But she decided that eating meat was not healthy for creatures from Vango 9."

"Okay," said Lily, "I'm going to bed. Eating all that ice cream has worn me out."

"Me too," said Klatu. "I am exalted."

The three Looglings and Lily all climbed into their beds. They fell asleep almost as soon as their heads hit the pillows.

Lily dreamed of sheep.

Ploo dreamed of home.

Lek dreamed of monsters.

And Klatu? Klatu dreamed of ice cream, especially the yummy stick part.

Looglish
Dictionary

arp: a unit of time, about an hour in Earth time; there are 50 *mynts* in an *arp*

crozzfozzn: wazoo, as in "stick things up our *crozzfozzn*"

Darksiders: Looglings who live on the Darkside of Loogl

esping: talking through E.S.P.

flumkins: parts of Loogling bodies, as in "They may pull the *flumkins* out of our *shtoosies!*"

foofoo: what Looglings make in the bathroom

Gamma Wormhole: a wormhole in space that enables Looglings to bypass an entire galaxy

gorin: a unit of money, as in a 50-*gorin* platinum coin

grabble: a griddle, as in "like *patkas* on a hot *grabble*"

Great Ones, the: Org, Murkel, Shemp, and Kurth—famous Loogling heroes who crashed in Roswell, New Mexico, in 1947

Gromple: Mars

hide-a-craft: a remote-control device that makes spacecraft invisible

"Jumping *jeblonskies!*": a Looglish expression of excitement

karpas: some kind of Looglish food

ketzelongo: a Looglish cat

klopotskis: bodily organs Looglings use for breathing

language gum: gum balls that, when chewed, allow a Loogling to speak a specific language

Lightsiders: Looglings who live on the Lightside of Loogl

Loogl: their home planet

"Looglings *laroosh loglaroohoo!*": a Looglish farewell

Looglphone: a Looglish cell phone

Mardoolian Bonklebob: a very fast spaceship from planet Mardoo

mynts: a unit of time, equal to about one Earth minute; there are 50 *mynts* in an *arp*

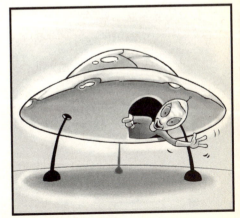

osster egg: the large egg of a Looglish ostrich-like bird

patkas: round, flat Looglish food cooked on a *grabble*

shmendler: a Looglish weapon that looks like a giant hamburger

shmerdlik: a dreadful Looglish animal

shtoosies: parts of Loogling bodies, as in "They may pull the *flumkins* out of our *shtoosies!*"

sikken: a unit of time, about a second in Earth time; there are 50 *sikkens* in a *mynt*

Snargle-ploom: something Loogling moms get mad if you're late for

varna: a moron, as in "You *varna!*"

vonko: crazy

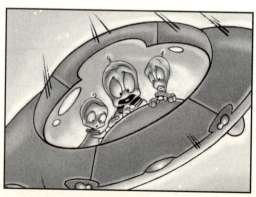